Diego's Manatee Rescue

by Sheila Sweeny Higginson   illustrated by Warner McGee

Simon Spotlight/Nickelodeon
New York   London   Toronto   Sydney

Based on the TV series *Go, Diego, Go!*™ as seen on Nick Jr.®

SIMON SPOTLIGHT
An imprint of Simon & Schuster Children's Publishing Division
1230 Avenue of the Americas, New York, New York 10020
© 2009 Viacom International Inc. All rights reserved.
NICK JR., *Go, Diego, Go!*, and all related titles, logos, and characters are trademarks of Viacom International Inc.
All rights reserved, including the right of reproduction in whole or in part in any form.
SIMON SPOTLIGHT and colophon are registered trademarks of Simon & Schuster, Inc.
Manufactured in the United States of America
First Edition
2 4 6 8 10 9 7 5 3 1
ISBN: 978-1-4169-7863-3

¡Hola! I'm Diego, and I'm an Animal Rescuer.
This is my sister Alicia.
Did you hear that squeaking sound? It sounds like an animal in trouble. Let's find out who it is!

Click the Camera can help us find out which animal is in trouble. Say "Click!"
Look! Click has four pictures of animals. The animal that needs our help says,
"Squeak, squeak."

Do you see an animal like that?
¡Sí! It's a manatee!
Alicia says that manatees live in the Mangrove Forest.
¡Al rescate, mis amigos! Let's rescue the manatee!

There are so many animals living in the Mangrove Forest. I see bats, crocodiles, and snakes.

Do you see them too? *¡Excelente!*

What other animals do you see living here? Yes—tree frogs, monkeys, and sloths.

But where's the manatee?

We need to help the manatee get down the river without getting hurt by the boat. But what can we use to go down the river?

Rescue Pack can transform into anything we need. Just say "*¡Actívate!*"

What can we use to get down the river?

¡Sí! We can use a raft to get down the river.
We have to stay away from the waves, or our raft could flip over.
Will you find a path that will get us safely down the river?
¡Sí! That's the way to go!

Look who's driving the motorboat! It's the Bobo Brothers.
We need to stop them!
Clap your hands three times. Then shout "Freeze, Bobos!"

The Bobo Brothers are sorry. Those silly monkeys didn't know that their motorboat could hurt the manatees. They promise to use a rowboat when they explore the river from now on.

The manatee calf is very hungry. We need to help her find some food.
Manatees eat plants—lots of them. Manatees can eat more than one hundred
pounds of plants in a day. That's like eating two hundred heads of lettuce!
Do you see some water plants for the manatee? *¡Perfecto!*

We're very close now, but there's a tree blocking the river. We're going to have to put on our diving gear and swim with the manatee.

Manatees can twist and turn their bodies in the water.
Let's twist and turn like manatees to get through the tree branches!

We helped the little manatee get to her mother! She is so happy!

¡Hola, Mami Manatee!

Now that *Mami* Manatee and her baby are together again, let's find them a nice, safe home away from any boats.

Let's look for a new home for our manatee friends. Click the Camera can help. Just say "Click! Take a pic!"

Click has four pictures of animal habitats.

The manatees live in shady water in the Mangrove Forest. Do you see a habitat like that?

¡Sí! You found the shady cove! My Field Journal shows that we can follow the river to get there.

Let's call the manatees to let them know they should follow us. Call with me. "Squeak, squeak!"

Now we need to find the river path that leads to the forest. Which path should we take?

¡Sí! The path is to the left!

We brought the manatees to their new home. They're so happy. They're rolling and playing in the water! They're so graceful!

¡Misión cumplida! Rescue complete!
Thanks for helping! *¡Gracias!*

Field Journal Facts

SOMETHING'S NOT FISHY.

Manatees may live in the water like fish, but they're mammals like whales, dolphins, elephants, or cows. That's one reason why the manatee is called the sea cow!

HOLD IT!

Manatees can hold their breath for twenty minutes when they are resting.

SALAD, ANYONE?

Manatees are herbivores. That means they graze on plants they find in the water.

UNDERWATER ACROBATS!

Manatees are huge, but they are very graceful. In the water, they can roll, turn, and somersault like acrobats.

MANATEES ARE ENDANGERED ANIMALS.

That means we need to do all we can to protect them.